FAN OF FROG-FRIENDLY FICTION

childrensfunnybooks.co.uk

THE FROG WHO WAS BLUE

THE FROG WHO WAS BLUE

FAIZ KERMANI

ILLUSTRATED BY NAOMI POWELL

Matador
9 Priory Business Park,
Wistow Road, Kibworth Beauchamp,
Leicestershire. LE8 0RX
Tel: 0116 279 2299
Email: books@troubador.co.uk
Web: www.troubador.co.uk/matador
Twitter: @matadorbooks

ISBN 978 1785899 959

British Library Cataloguing in Publication Data.
A catalogue record for this book is available from the British Library.

Printed and bound by CPI Group (UK) Ltd, Croydon, CR0 4YY
Typeset in 14pt Aldine 401 BT by Troubador Publishing Ltd, Leicester, UK

Matador is an imprint of Troubador Publishing Ltd

Dedicated to all friends of
The World Medical Fund.

Deep in Malawi, in the warm heart of Africa, lay Lake Ticklewater. It was the home of many creatures, but especially frogs, who lived there among the stones and wild plants. No one could remember why, but the Lake Ticklewater frogs were all blue. Apart from that, they were ordinary frogs.

One day, however, one of these ordinary frogs received an extraordinary piece of news: he had won a place at Croak College, the most famous school for frogs in Malawi! The name of this lucky frog was Biriwita.

Biriwita had always dreamed of going to Croak College, but he had never before left the lake. He knew that he was going to miss his friends and family.

After a tiring swim across the lake, Biriwita finally spotted a sign. It read:

CROAK COLLEGE –
MALAWI'S FINEST SCHOOL
FOR THE FINEST FROGS.

At the school gates, a teacher welcomed Biriwita and immediately showed him to his first class, which was being held by an upside-down tree at the top of a small hill.

Biriwita tried to talk to the other frogs, but as soon as they saw him they started to laugh.

“Yuck – you’re blue! How weird!” they said.

Biriwita tried to defend himself. “All the Lake Ticklewater frogs are blue,” he replied. “What’s wrong with that?”

“Blue is a stupid colour,” they said. “Why aren’t you green like us?”

Biriwita could not think of what to say. He felt sad.

When the class ended, Biriwita tried to leave as quickly as possible, but a large group of frogs blocked his way. They started to make fun of him and pushed him around.

"Why can't you be green like a normal frog?" they laughed.

"Do all frogs in Lake Ticklewater look as strange as you?" they joked.

They gathered around Biriwita and started to sing a nasty song.

WHAT'S WRONG WITH YOU?
WHY ARE YOU BLUE?
YOU'RE THE STRANGEST FROG WE'VE SEEN
NORMAL FROGS ARE GREEN!

Biriwita was too scared of the other frogs to sleep in the school dormitory that night. He hid in a small hole near the hill and covered himself with grass to keep warm. He was upset because his first day at school had been a disaster. Why were the other frogs so mean to him?

The next day, Biriwita waited in his hole until it was time to come out for class. When he reached the top of the hill he found that the other frogs were waiting for him.

“Look! It’s the funny blue frog,” they shouted. Biriwita tried to hop away from them but they started to push and kick him.

That evening, Biriwita sat on the rock by the upside-down tree and watched the frogs jumping about in the water below. What fun it looked! He wished he could join them.

Out of the corner of his eye, he noticed a dark shape sticking out of the water. None of the frogs had seen it, but Biriwita immediately thought that it looked strange. Why would a piece of wood move from side to side?

While the frogs were swimming in circles, laughing and chasing each other, Biriwita suddenly realised what he was looking at. Unlike these frogs, everyone who lived in Lake Ticklewater knew when a crocodile was planning an attack!

Biriwita shouted from the top of the hill, but none of the frogs took any notice of him. When he screamed louder and jumped up and down some of the frogs spotted him and started singing their nasty song again.

WHAT'S WRONG WITH YOU?
WHY ARE YOU BLUE?
YOU'RE THE STRANGEST FROG WE'VE SEEN
NORMAL FROGS ARE GREEN!

Desperately, Biriwita tried to think of a plan. He had to stop the crocodile! What could he do?

He crouched down behind the rock he had been sitting on and, using all his strength, pushed it away from the upside-down tree.

PLOP!

Biriwita fell over as the rock moved away from him. It began to roll down the hill toward the river, picking up speed. But the crocodile had nearly reached the frogs.

As the crocodile leaped out of the water with its jaws open wide, the frogs realised what was happening and screamed in terror. It was too late for them to get away. But right at that moment, the rock Biriwita had sent rolling down the hill flew into the crocodile's open mouth.

The crocodile had always enjoyed eating frogs, but it was not used to the taste of a dusty rock. The force of the rock smashing through its front teeth and landing on its tongue gave the huge creature a big surprise.

"Aargh! Aargh!" groaned the crocodile in pain. It swam off, thrashing its tail and coughing.

The noise had brought everyone else from the school to the river. They were shocked by what had happened. Everyone felt very ashamed about how they had behaved. It was only thanks to Biriwita's bravery that the frogs had been saved from the crocodile. One by one, all the frogs apologised.

"Please forgive us, Biriwita," said the frogs. "We hope that you will want to continue studying with us at Croak College."

Biriwita soon became the most popular frog in the school. No one cared that he was blue any more. Everyone wanted to talk to him and hear the exciting story about how he had stopped the crocodile.

A few weeks later, everyone gathered for the graduation ceremony. Biriwita's family waved to him from the crowd. He would be the first frog from Lake Ticklewater to graduate from Croak College!

After the main ceremony the teacher made an announcement for the best student award. "We are delighted to give this special award to Biriwita – the bravest frog in all of Malawi!"

Biriwita proudly held up the silver cup. Everyone cheered and congratulated him.

As the sun set that evening, Biriwita and all the other frogs had a big party by the river to celebrate.

He laughed as his friends sang their new song:

WHO CARES IF YOU'RE NOT GREEN
YOU'RE THE BRAVEST FROG WE'VE SEEN
EVERYONE KNOWS IT'S TRUE
THAT THE FINEST FROGS ARE BLUE!

ABOUT THE WORLD MEDICAL FUND (WMF)

The World Medical Fund (WMF) is a medical charity working in Africa. Our focus is on Africa's poorest and most vulnerable children, including AIDS orphans. Every day we save young lives and ease suffering by making medical care available to village children, often for the first time.

WMF was founded with two key objectives: high achievement on the ground and low administration costs. To date we have managed to do this, but we urgently need more funds and other assistance to ensure that WMF is able to maintain its battle against malaria and save children's lives.

For more information, please visit www.worldmedicalfund.org

ABOUT THE AUTHOR

Faiz Kermani is an award-winning British author who lives with his family in France.

For more information on his books, please visit www.childrensfunnybooks.co.uk.

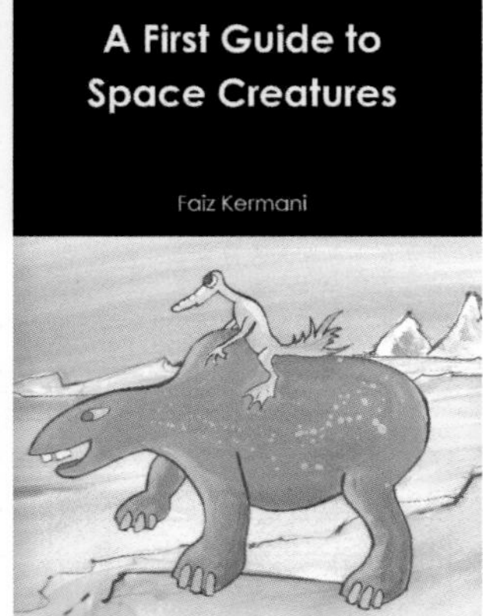

ABOUT THE ILLUSTRATOR

Naomi Powell recently graduated from the University of Gloucestershire with a degree in Illustration. Originally from North Devon, she's worked in reportage style all over the world, and works from her sketches to create new work. Her work incorporated a combination of digital and mixed media. She has an affinity for cats, and is about to embark on her Masters degree in Illustration.

For more information on her work, please visit www. naomipowell.com.